DISNEY'S
THE HUNCHBACK OF NOTRE DAME

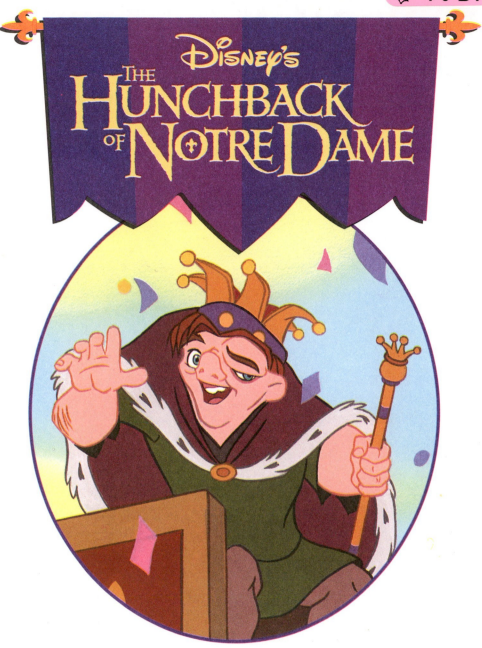

Adapted by Justine Korman
Illustrated by Don Williams

A GOLDEN BOOK • NEW YORK
Western Publishing Company, Inc., Racine, Wisconsin 53404

Once upon a time, in the city of Paris, a young man lived in the bell tower of Notre Dame cathedral. He was strong enough to ring the giant church bells, but he was also so gentle he could hold a young bird in his hand. His only friends were three gargoyles. They didn't mind that he had a hunchback and a face so ugly that his cruel master named him Quasimodo, which means "half-formed."

Quasimodo knew nothing of the world below his tower, except what his master, Judge Frollo, told him. Frollo hated everyone—especially the gypsies. He had even taught Quasimodo to think of himself as a monster.

Quasimodo spent his lonely days ringing the bells and carving small wooden figures. He longed to see the world, but Frollo wouldn't let him leave the bell tower. This was Quasimodo's great sorrow, for he wanted so much to join the crowds in the streets of Paris.

Once a year everyone in Paris celebrated the Festival of Fools. On that topsy-turvy day, Quasimodo's gargoyle friends encouraged him to climb down from the tower and join in the fun. During the festival, many people wore masks, so no one paid any attention to Quasimodo's looks.

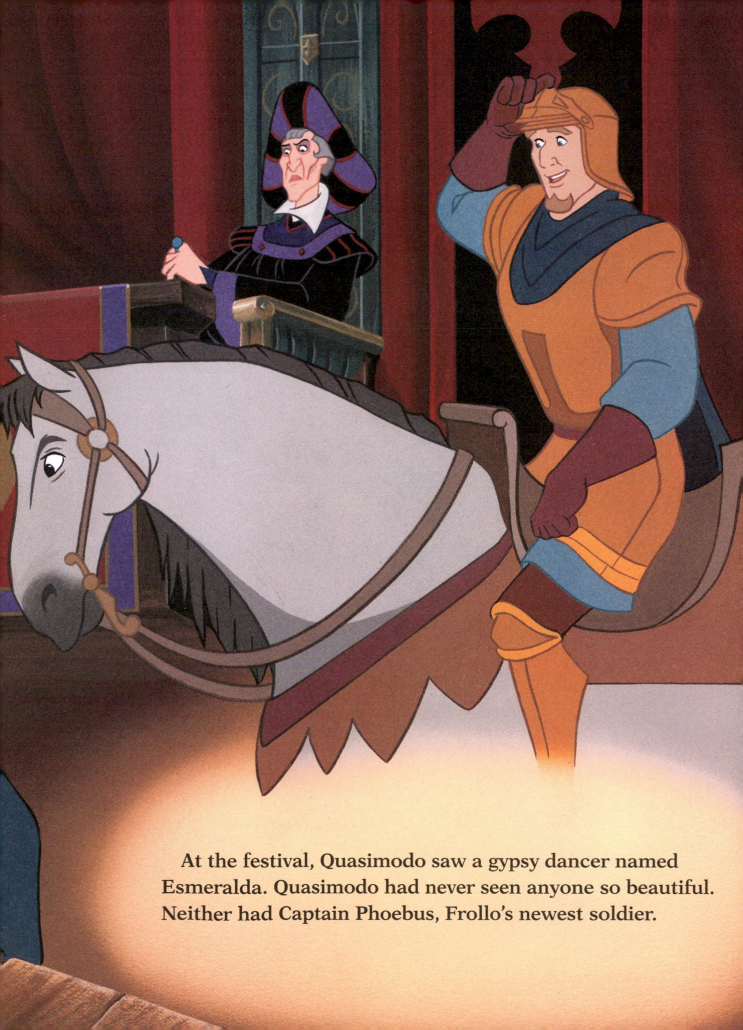

At the festival, Quasimodo saw a gypsy dancer named Esmeralda. Quasimodo had never seen anyone so beautiful. Neither had Captain Phoebus, Frollo's newest soldier.

Suddenly the crowd grabbed Quasimodo and crowned him King of Fools. All the people cheered—until they found out his face was not a mask!

"He's a monster!" they jeered, and threw ropes over him so he couldn't get away.

Desperately Quasimodo begged Frollo for help. But he refused.

Kindhearted Esmeralda set Quasimodo free. "You mistreat this poor boy just as you mistreat my people," she said to Frollo. Then she tossed the King of Fools' crown at Frollo's feet.

"You will pay for this!" Frollo said angrily. "Captain Phoebus, arrest her!"

But Esmeralda sneaked into Notre Dame with her goat, Djali. Captain Phoebus found her there, but he did not want to arrest her. He told Esmeralda to claim sanctuary—the right to protection as long as she stayed inside the cathedral.

"Set one foot outside these walls and you're my prisoner!" Frollo declared.

Quasimodo was confused. Frollo had told him all gypsies were evil. But Esmeralda was kind and good. She did not think Quasimodo was a monster. "Maybe Frollo is wrong about both of us," Esmeralda said.

Quasimodo decided to help her escape.

Very quietly Quasimodo carried Esmeralda and Djali down the cathedral walls to the street.

Esmeralda pressed a special amulet into Quasimodo's hand. "Use this if you ever need help," she said. "It will show you how to find the gypsy hideout—the Court of Miracles." Then she kissed Quasimodo on the cheek and promised to visit him again.

And soon she did—with Phoebus. When Esmeralda had escaped, Frollo was furious. He had ordered his men to arrest all the gypsies. Phoebus had refused, and was badly wounded for defying Frollo.

"Please keep Phoebus here until he's strong again," Esmeralda begged Quasimodo as Frollo approached. So Quasimodo agreed to hide Phoebus in the bell tower, and Esmeralda hurried away.

Frollo thought Quasimodo might know how to find Esmeralda
and the other gypsies. "I know where her hideout is," he told
Quasimodo. "I will attack at dawn with a thousand men."
But it was a trick!

Using Esmeralda's amulet to find the Court of Miracles, Quasimodo and Phoebus rushed to warn the gypsies. But Frollo's men had secretly been following them! The hateful judge had finally caught up with the gypsies.

"Take them away!" Frollo cried.
Quasimodo fell at his master's feet. "No, please!" he begged.
But Frollo's heart was as hard as the stones of Notre Dame.

The next day Quasimodo was chained high in the cathedral. In the square below, Frollo threatened to punish Esmeralda.

"*Noooo!*" Quasimodo cried. He strained at his chains until they broke. Then he scrambled down the walls.

He freed Esmeralda and carried her up to safety in the cathedral tower.

"Break down the door!" Frollo commanded. But Phoebus and the people of Paris would not let anyone hurt their beloved Notre Dame. The gargoyles also helped Quasimodo defend the church against Frollo and his men. Finally Frollo was defeated.

At long last Frollo's evil reign had ended. The crowd cheered, "Hip, hip, hooray for Quasimodo!"

Finally Quasimodo understood that he wasn't a monster at all. To the people of Paris, he was a great hero!